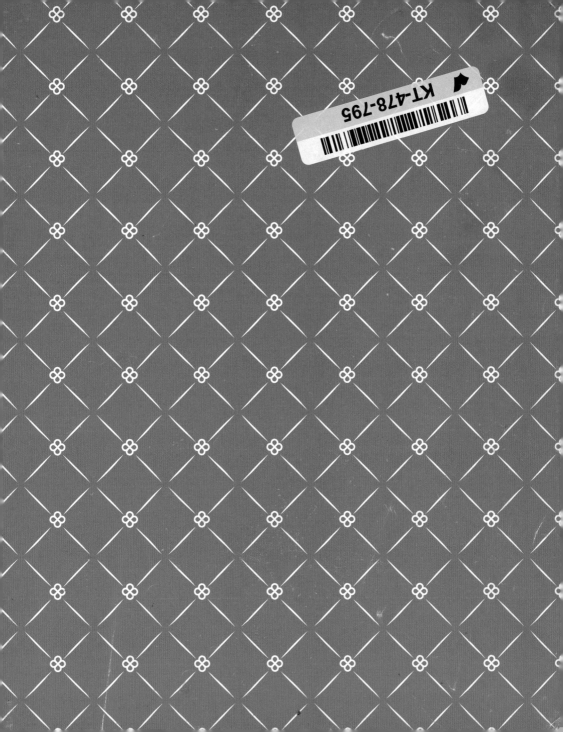
KT-478-795

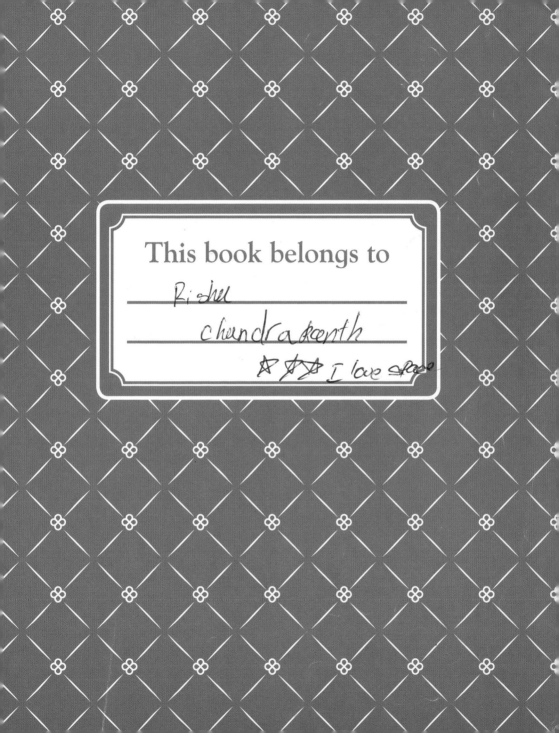

This book belongs to

Rishu

chandrakenth

☆ ☆☆ I love ♥♥♥

This edition published by Parragon Books Ltd in 2015

Parragon Books Ltd
Chartist House
15–17 Trim Street
Bath BA1 1HA, UK
www.parragon.com

Copyright © 2015 Disney Enterprises, Inc.

All rights reserved. No part of this publication may be reproduced, stored in a retrieval system or transmitted, in any form or by any means, electronic, mechanical, photocopying, recording or otherwise, without the prior permission of the copyright holder.

ISBN 978-1-4748-0652-7

Printed in China

DISNEY MOVIE COLLECTION
A CLASSIC DISNEY STORYBOOK SERIES

Cinderella

PaRragon
Bath • New York • Cologne • Melbourne • Delhi
Hong Kong • Shenzhen • Singapore • Amsterdam

Once upon a time, there lived a beautiful girl called Cinderella. Her mother had died when she was very young so Cinderella lived alone with her father. She loved her father dearly but he knew that his daughter needed a mother, so he married again. Cinderella's stepmother had two daughters of her own, Drizella and Anastasia.

But when her father died suddenly, a broken-hearted
Cinderella quickly discovered that her stepmother,
Lady Tremaine, was cold, cruel and bitterly jealous of
Cinderella's charm and beauty.

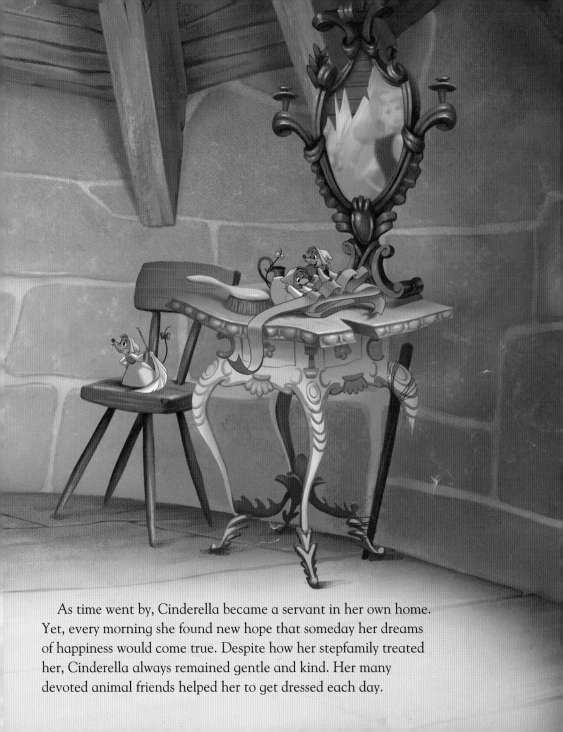

As time went by, Cinderella became a servant in her own home.
Yet, every morning she found new hope that someday her dreams
of happiness would come true. Despite how her stepfamily treated
her, Cinderella always remained gentle and kind. Her many
devoted animal friends helped her to get dressed each day.

One morning, Jaq the mouse rushed in to tell
Cinderella that a new mouse was caught in a trap!
Cinderella hurried down to the cellar to rescue him.
"The poor little thing is scared to death!" Cinderella said.
"Jaq, maybe you'd better explain things to him."

Jaq befriended the new mouse and Cinderella gave
him a shirt, shoes, cap – and a name. "We'll call you
Gus," she said.

Gus giggled his approval.

Among her many chores, Cinderella had to go to the farmyard to feed the chickens. The mice always followed her because Cinderella saved some corn for them every day.

But today, Lady Tremaine's mean old cat, Lucifer, was blocking their way! The mice drew tails to see who would distract Lucifer so the others could run outside.

It was up to Jaq! He quietly crept up to Lucifer and kicked the cat's leg out from under him. SPLASH! Lucifer slipped face down into his milk bowl and the mice scurried past and out into the farmyard.

Cinderella had been wondering where the mice were. "Breakfast is served," she said when they appeared, and she scattered plump kernels of corn on the ground for them.

Cinderella spent the rest of her day attending to chores.

"Take that ironing," Drizella demanded.

"Don't forget to make our tea," Anastasia added.

"Pick up the laundry and get on with your duties," her stepmother ordered.

Meanwhile, at the royal palace, the King complained to the Grand Duke. "It's high time my son got married," he sobbed. "I want grandchildren!"

The King decided to hold a ball. "If all the eligible maidens come," said the King, "the Prince is bound to find his bride among them."

Later that morning, Cinderella paused from her chores to answer a knock at the door. A palace messenger handed her an invitation to the ball for that very evening.

Her stepmother grabbed the invitation and read it aloud. "By royal command, every eligible maiden is to attend," she said.

Her daughters squealed with excitement.

"I'm so eligible!" said Anastasia.

They both imagined the Prince would fall in love with them.

Cinderella was also excited. "Why, that means I can go, too!" she said.

The stepsisters laughed. "Every eligible maiden is supposed to attend," said Cinderella.

Surprisingly, her stepmother agreed. "I don't see why you can't go ... *if* you get all your work done, and *if* you can find something suitable to wear."

Cinderella raced to her room and found a dress that had belonged to her mother. With a little stitching, she knew she could make it pretty.

As Cinderella worked on the dress, her stepmother and stepsisters called for her and gave her a long list of chores to do.

Meanwhile, the mice and the birds retrieved some sashes and beads that the stepsisters had thrown away. With some clever stitching and folding, they turned Cinderella's simple dress into a fabulous ballgown!

Cinderella finally finished her chores and went up to her room. She was so sad when she saw how late it was and realized she had no time to mend her dress before the ball. She gazed out of the window. In the distance, she could just make out the long line of carriages arriving at the palace for the ball.

Then, out of the corner of her eye,
Cinderella saw her new dress.

"Surprise!" yelled the mice and birds.

"Oh, thank you so much!" Cinderella cried
with delight.

When Anastasia and Drizella saw Cinderella looking so beautiful in their old sashes and beads, they flew into a jealous rage.

They ripped Cinderella's dress, pulling off the sashes and yanking the beads, while Lady Tremaine just stood and watched.

Now Cinderella had no hope at all of making it to the ball. She ran to the garden and sobbed. "There's nothing left to believe in," she said, "nothing."

But just then, a comforting presence appeared beside her – it was Cinderella's Fairy Godmother. "Dry those tears," she told Cinderella. "You can't go to the ball looking like that."

"But I'm not going," said Cinderella.

"Of course you are," replied the Fairy Godmother.

The Fairy Godmother waved her magic wand
over a pumpkin and a regal coach appeared!
"Oh, it's beautiful," said Cinderella.
Then the Fairy Godmother turned Jaq and Gus
and two other mice into four beautiful white horses.
She changed Major the horse into the coach driver
and Bruno the dog into the footman.

The Fairy Godmother waved her wand again and said
"Bibbidi-bobbidi-boo!" With that, she turned Cinderella's
torn dress into a beautiful gown. Then a pair of dainty glass
slippers appeared on Cinderella's feet.

"On the stroke of midnight, the spell will be broken," the
Fairy Godmother warned, "and everything will be as before."

Cinderella raced to the palace in her magical carriage,
her friends carrying her as fast as they possibly could.

Every maiden at the ball came forward in turn to meet the Prince, including Anastasia and Drizella.

The sisters curtsied before the Prince but he was not looking at them – he had noticed Cinderella standing behind them.

The Prince hurried over to Cinderella, eager
to meet the most beautiful girl he had ever seen.
They talked for a while and then the Prince
led Cinderella into the ballroom.

They danced and danced, gazing deeply into
each other's eyes ... the two were falling in love.

But suddenly the clock began to strike midnight. BONG! BONG!
"I must go!" Cinderella cried in panic, freeing her hand from the Prince's.
As she fled, she lost one of her glass slippers on the staircase.

Cinderella jumped into her waiting carriage. They were a short distance from the palace when the clock finished striking. Everyone and everything turned back to normal! But Cinderella still had one glass slipper. She looked up and thanked her Fairy Godmother for a magical evening.

Back at the Palace, the Prince vowed that he would marry the girl who had lost her glass slipper at the ball.

The King was furious that the girl his son now loved had vanished and nobody seemed to know who she was. He demanded that the Grand Duke go and find her.

A royal messenger brought news of the search to Lady Tremaine. She read the notice aloud – the Prince would marry whoever fitted the glass slipper. Anastasia and Drizella were excited to have another chance to marry the Prince.

Cinderella overheard her stepmother reading the royal message and ran to her room, not quite believing what she had heard. The Prince had fallen in love with her, just as she had fallen in love with him! But Lady Tremaine realized that it must have been Cinderella who had lost the slipper. She went up to Cinderella's room ...

... and locked the door!
"Let me out!" Cinderella cried.
But her stepmother put the key
in her pocket and left.

The Grand Duke travelled the kingdom on behalf of the King, searching for the owner of the glass slipper. When he arrived at Lady Tremaine's house, she and her daughters hurried to greet him.

Meanwhile, Jaq and Gus had seen what the stepmother had done to Cinderella. So, while she was talking to the Grand Duke, they sneaked up and stole the key from her pocket!

They took it back to Cinderella and slid it under her door.

The Grand Duke looked on as his footman tried to squeeze
Anastasia's and Drizella's huge feet into the delicate little slipper.
Of course, it did not fit either of them.

Just as the Grand Duke was about to leave,
Cinderella appeared at the top of the stairs.
Her animal friends had freed her just in time!
"May I try on the slipper?" she asked.

The angry stepmother tripped the footman as he approached Cinderella. The glass slipper shattered on the floor.

"Oh, no!" moaned the Grand Duke.

"But you see," said Cinderella, reaching into her pocket, "I have the other slipper." Quickly, the Grand Duke put the slipper on Cinderella's foot.

It fitted perfectly! Cinderella was the Prince's love!

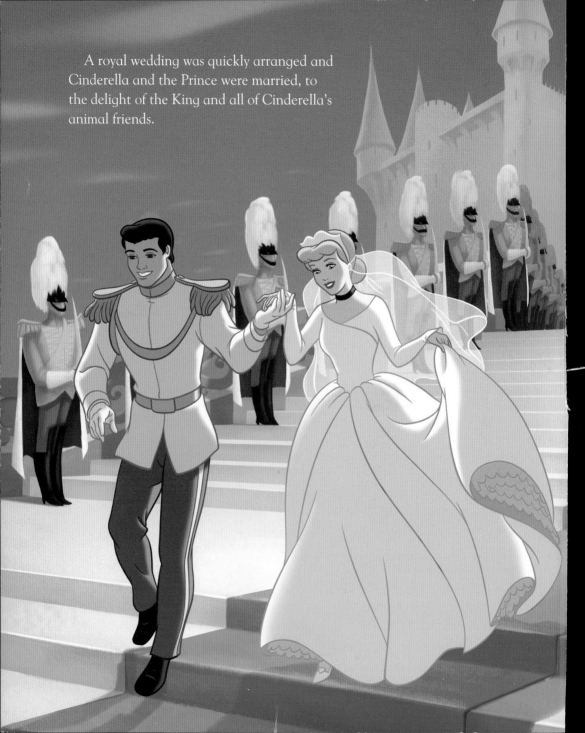

A royal wedding was quickly arranged and Cinderella and the Prince were married, to the delight of the King and all of Cinderella's animal friends.

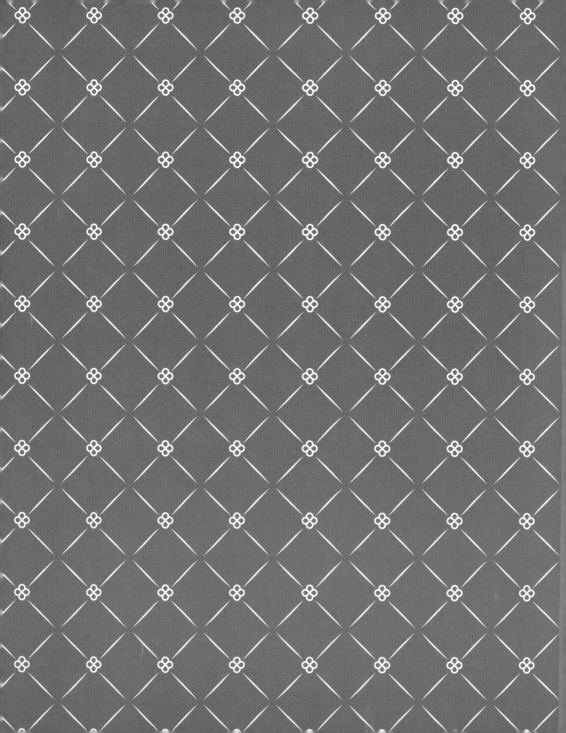